PREFACE TO THE FIRS

"Violists" began to germinate early in December last, as Christmas approached. I originally intended that it be ready before the new year, but alas, it came in behind schedule, and was not completed until January. It is still winter in some places—the right season for such morsels—so rather than let the work languish upon the shelf for another year...

Somewhere out there on The Net, I hope there is a solitary reader settled comfortably in a warm study with a nice cup of tea. Perhaps the lights are out, and the amber glow of the terminal spreads faint warmth through the room; overstuffed bookshelves loom behind in the darkness. If the evening air is crisp and a soft snow is falling outside the window, so much the better—a view of icicles would be a magical touch.

— Richard McGowan
San Jose, California
January 22, 1994

GRETCHEN IN THE LIBRARY

In winter the interior of the university library was hardly warmer than the outside, and it was terribly drafty. The sole difference between the interior and exterior, Gretchen often remarked to herself, was that the latter received an occasional snow. The library at least was dry. On most days in the unfrequented areas—the closed stacks on the second and third floors—one could see one's breath in the middle of the afternoon. Gretchen thought it hardly the sort of climate she would have chosen for her own books. But the cost of heating such an enormous building—well, she decided she could hardly imagine so extravagant a sum. On the coldest days, she often wore two petticoats. She found the best method of staying warm, though, was to bustle as quickly as she could. Primarily, she worked in the stacks, extracting books for the library's patrons and reshelving books that had returned—and keeping the shelves in good order.

Gretchen's twenty-ninth birthday had arrived—quite too quickly—the day before, and she bustled with an excess of alacrity to relieve her mind from the brooding that had occupied her for several days. She had spent the evening alone, though she knew it did her no good to seek solitude. To accept being past her prime of life would be simpler perhaps, and productive of less anguish, than fretting over what could not be changed. She was nearly thirty, though—and she knew what lay in store for her a few years hence. She had only to look at the assistant reference librarian, Miss Sadie, to see how she herself would be in but a few more years. The thought nearly made her shudder, and if she allowed herself to think too deeply upon the matter, might have brought her to tears. Thankfully, Gretchen told herself, she could grow old among the books, where at least she had the company of great minds—or their legacy—rather than spend a life straining in a factory—or under the yoke of an old-fashioned man.

She had been estranged from her family for six years and rarely given them serious thought since fleeing Connecticut. A simple enough row it had been to start—what should she do now that she had finished university? Of course her father recommended marriage and settling into the domestic life—a pretty girl like her. Him and his antiquated ideals—a pretty girl in the kitchen, indeed! At twenty-three she had finally come to her senses and refused to marry the young man to whom she had been betrothed, no matter how well matched her father thought they were.

Her mother had frequently confided to Gretchen her views on the varied pleasures—and trials—inherent in marriage, admitting that as the years passed she found the pleasures perhaps not worth the other hardships—the outward subjugation of her own feelings and the constant deference she was required to display within the confines of that marriage, as if she had no independent mind. Gretchen had long since determined that would not be her fate. She had come to believe that no suitable man could be found, yet she remained unsatisfied. The only true regret she had about casting off her family ties was that she had disappointed her mother. It was her mother who had worked so hard, really, to see that Gretchen had an education; her father only begrudgingly went along for the sake of domestic tranquility when all efforts to dissuade her had failed.

At university Gretchen had imbibed the rarefied intellectual atmosphere with increasing eagerness and found herself drawn irresistibly up the slopes of Parnassus. She had always intended to work after completing university—and work she did, though she had difficulty making due with what employment she could find. Even a superlative education, she had learned in six years, did not buy one certain rights or reasonable wages. She hoped that she would yet see the flowering of an age that she could call an enlightened one. She might have been bitter had she higher material aspirations, but she was content with little in the way of physical comforts. Why the privilege of spending nearly all her days in the library would have been worth almost any sacrifice—what need had she of wages!

It was lamentable, she decided, that she should have to forgo marital companionship if she were to retain her individuality—for the price of her freedom was a monumental sort of loneliness that only the severest mental discipline could overcome. She had seen so many of her school friends smothered in the clutches of bad marriages, worn out beneath their husbands' heels—almost like doormats. To be truthful there were those who seemed to prosper in the state of matrimony, but she thought them few. Yet, she still had an abiding fear that she would grow old alone—and soon enough become as obdurate as Miss Sadie—a pitiable spinster with none of the finer sensibilities left to her. Was there no man, Gretchen wondered, with whom she could share her life and interests—a man with progressive ideas? Not a man that she, like a tiny moon, would orbit eternally, but one with whom she could find a state of mutual orbit. Well, she thought, something of that nature anyway. Her knowledge of astronomy was not up to the task of finding a better analogy, and she resolved to remedy that as soon as she was able. She added another volume—'something concerning the heavens' she called it—to the list of books she thought she really must read.

Gretchen bustled, thinking these thoughts, dreading her next birthday. She blew softly on a wisp of auburn hair that had somehow escaped from the green ribbon with which she tied it back that morning. Several strands had somehow got into her mouth but her arms were too full of books—heavy tomes, all—to pull them away with her fingers. She was on the verge of setting down the burden and tending to her hair for a moment when, as she turned a corner into the next row, a shadow fell across the topmost book in her arms. She glanced up in surprise. A man stood mere inches in front of her—and looked up to find her bearing down upon him with a full head of steam—even as he stepped toward her.

"Oh!" she cried, attempting to stop herself. The books slid irretrievably from her grasp, their pages flying open with a flutter.

The man's arms shot out. "The books!" came his cry of astonishment as they tumbled about him. He tried to catch a few, left and then right, but alas they fell—all but one—to the floor with a dull clatter.

"Oh dear," Gretchen whispered, looking down. She feared she had bent a few pages, and putting a hand to her mouth knelt immediately to gather them all. "I'm terribly sorry, sir," she continued in a rush as she piled books one after the other. "My clumsiness..."

"Think nothing of it, Miss," the man replied lightly. "It's my fault. I do hope _you_ were not harmed by _my_ clumsiness..." He knelt then, and began to place books upon her stack, starting with the volume he had saved from falling. The lucky book was one of the late Mr. Darwin's, and when he glanced momentarily at the spine she blushed deeply despite herself—for she had that day finished reading it, and was returning it to its rightful place. She knew that he had seen her cheeks color.

Gretchen looked around, and seeing there were no more stray books, prepared to pick up the stack again. She stood up to catch her breath and smooth her wool skirt, arching back her shoulders. Looking down at the man, she finally remembered to blow the wisp of hair from her face. He was looking up at her and positively beaming—clean-shaven and light complected, she noted—but the smile faded almost instantly to a faint curling about the corners of his lips.

"Please accept my apologies," he stated, still kneeling upon the floor. "I will have to be more careful." His hair was dishevelled—great curly locks of jet black, and he laughed nervously as he brushed it from his eyes. He peered at her with eyes so black, yet so kindly, that Gretchen found herself blushing again and put a hand to her chest. The man stopped for a moment to adjust his shirt and coat, then stood slowly, and with the hint of a bow, swept past her and away. Unaccountably, she felt suddenly light-headed and sat down upon the floor by her books. His eyes! she exclaimed to herself with an outrush of breath. She felt that in an instant they had devoured her; had known all about her. She could not recall ever having seen such lively and intelligent eyes—so deep and black they seemed like windows opening onto a starlit sky. And his hand! when he placed the last book upon the stack—

the nails so trim. His hands were almost feminine, and finely wrought. Gretchen gradually composed herself, then picked up her books and continued about her work.

Several times thereafter in the course of a fortnight Gretchen saw the same young man about the library, and they developed an acquaintance that began and ended with nodding pleasantly and wishing each other "good day". She thought him quite the most interesting patron she had seen in the library for... she knew not how long—perhaps never in the two years she had been there. He was flamboyant, certainly, Gretchen decided, but he had not that rakishness or arrogance that so often accompanies one who is as smart a dresser as he seemed. Her thoughts chanced to light upon him sometimes, and within the fortnight, she decided he must be attached to the university. Perhaps a professor—well certainly not a full professor, he was far too young and had not grown into that masculine stuffiness that comes with long tenure—and his physique was trim. No, she decided, he was probably a fresh young assistant to an elder professor.

"Gretchen, dear." Miss Sadie's voice crackled behind her in a very strange manner and Gretchen looked around. "I do fear I'm catching some contagion, dear," Miss Sadie continued in a whisper, "can you possibly mind the desk until closing?"

Gretchen hesitated for a moment. She had worked long enough in the library to feel at ease, and with classes already in recess for the Christmas holidays, there were few patrons. "Of course, Miss Sadie," she answered. "I do hope you're feeling better tomorrow."

"If not, I shan't be in," Miss Sadie replied in a very weak tone. "I'll—I'll try to send word."

"I'll see to everything, Miss Sadie—just take care of yourself." She paused. "And I'll inform Mr. Johnson—it's no trouble at all." With a smile and a pitying wag of her head, she added, "Take good care of yourself."

Miss Sadie thanked her, and took her leave. Gretchen was alone, at last, if only for an evening, as temporary queen of the reference desk. Well, it was about time she was asked to do something besides fetch books, she thought airily, and took a seat at Miss Sadie's desk. Miss Sadie was not very neat for a librarian, she thought, wiping a finger across the desk, so she began to tidy a few things up. She put down a fresh blotter and arranged the papers in a more orderly manner, then opened a drawer in search of a cloth. Really, Miss Sadie is the epitome of disorganization, she muttered, seeing the jumble. It's a wonder that a woman like her can retain such a position.

Bing-bing! Gretchen looked up suddenly when the bell upon the front counter sounded. Standing there with his hand poised above the bell was the young man.

"May I be of assistance?" Gretchen asked, in her most librarian-like tone.

The young man smiled. "I sincerely hope you can. I wonder if you might be able to help me find this book?" He held out a small slip of paper between two fingers. "It doesn't appear to be in the open stacks."

Gretchen glided to the desk and took the slip of paper from him. A glance at the number was sufficient. "You're correct," she told him, handing the paper back. "It's in one of the special collections."

"I wonder, then, Miss..." He paused, drawing out the word into a silence, until Gretchen felt obliged to fill the audible gap.

"Haviland," she offered in a whisper.

"Miss Haviland. Could you help me locate it?" He smiled with the slightly curling lips he always wore. Not condescending, she decided—perhaps amused, or even flirtatious.

Gretchen stood flustered for a moment. Patrons were not allowed into the special collections—they were under lock and key. Should she leave the reference desk unattended while she fetched it for him? In the interim, what if another patron had pressing business? A preposterous quandary, Gretchen then told herself. "Of course, Professor," she replied crisply. "Let me bring the key."

The young man laughed then, with a toss of his head so that his black curls flopped into his eyes. He suddenly sighed, with an exaggerated look of defeat, brushing back his hair. "Do I appear so like a professor, Miss Haviland? How did you know?"

It was Gretchen's turn to be amused, and she smiled as she went to Miss Sadie's desk drawer to bring the key. "You have not the air of a student, Professor..." she drew out the word in a manner imitative of his previous query, until he had to break into a wondrous smile.

"Bridwell!" he exclaimed, and rapped four fingernails once upon the desk. "Employed only this year—in the English department."

"Professor Bridwell," she continued, imparting a certain air of coquetry to her words, "your dress is frankly too punctilious for a student; and if I might be so tactless, you seem... more evolved, shall we say."

Having drawn out the key, she beckoned him to follow. They ascended the back staircase—likewise taboo for patrons. All the while Gretchen thought how to exonerate herself should she be caught by one of her superiors while leading a patron—alone—into the inner sanctum. She decided the best approach would be to plead ignorance—"Oh," she could say, "I had no idea that professors were considered ordinary patrons." Would that be sufficient excuse?

The book was easy to find, and Gretchen put herself to no particular difficulty—but nevertheless, Professor Bridwell's thanks were profuse. He consulted the book—which could not leave the library—for an hour or more. On departing he returned the book to the counter. He inclined his head, with the now-familiar flop of his curly hair, and said, "I do hope to have the pleasure again, Miss Haviland."

Gretchen watched from Miss Sadie's desk as he departed through the foyer and down the steps leading out. She closed her eyes for a moment and sat quietly after he had left—simply savoring the moment. A faint scent lingered behind him: a distinctive cologne that left quite a favorable impression on her.

Gretchen attended a short afternoon concert on campus. It was the last student recital of the season, and she had heard tell of the program: the afternoon was to open with mazurkas by Chopin and a selection of those divine "Transcendental Etudes" by Liszt—she could not stay away. Chopin was an aperitif, followed by a few mildly diverting piano works by students. Then, she sat breathless and transported—utterly transported, halfway to tears upon a bed of clouds—through the etudes of Liszt. In particular she had never heard the "Harmonies du Soir" more beautifully rendered.

After an intermission, which she spent simply sitting quietly, pondering the exquisite delicacies of Liszt's piano writing, the second part of the concert opened with Vivaldi's "The Four Seasons", performed by an intimate ensemble rather than with the full complement of strings. The performers were students, to be sure, but she found it delightful nonetheless. When the "Autumn" season opened, she even felt a sudden chill in the air—the performance was so wonderfully effective—and she pulled her shawl more tightly around her shoulders. She chanced then to look across the audience, and thought that several rows down, in front of her, she saw Professor Bridwell. She had no idea he liked concerts; in fact, she realized that she knew nothing whatever about him. She was positive it was the professor—even from the back, there was no mistaking his curly hair. At once she realized that he rather resembled portraits of Hector Berlioz. He sat upright, almost leaning forward in a posture that seemed ready to rise in an instant. She fancied that could she but see his handsome face, his eyes would be closed, as he was carried away by the music, blown upon Vivaldi's autumn wind.

Why she was looking at the audience rather than at the orchestra she really did not know—she forced her gaze away from the professor's back and tried to concentrate again upon the music. But her effort was unsuccessful.

When the concert was ended, Gretchen fairly ran to the exit, and stood there at the door, looking back across the auditorium. Yes, it was he, she saw finally. He was coming up the aisle and she glimpsed his face among the swarm of bodies. He appeared to be alone; he spoke to nobody. She stepped out of the way and kept looking across the audience, as if seeking someone else. He soon arrived, and when he walked past, she turned and looked at him, as if suddenly noticing him for the first time.

His smile was as delightful as always. "Good evening, Miss Haviland," he said, with a tone of warmth.

"Good evening, Professor." Gretchen thought that he slowed for a second or two, but she felt acutely embarrassed to be observing him too closely, and looked away toward the crowd again. He continued walking.

When the professor had passed, Gretchen let out her breath slowly. Into the thick of the crowd she plunged, and went out through the lobby. Evening had come on and it was dark outside. Vast hordes were dispersing across the plaza, pouring from the auditorium. As she stepped into the bitterly chill air and started down the stairs, a voice hailed her from behind.

"Are you alone, then, Miss Haviland?"

Gretchen whirled around at the sound of the professor's voice, in time to see him laugh briefly. He was standing just outside the doors, facing outward, his greatcoat pulled tightly around himself.

Gretchen went to stand on the step below. "Actually, yes," she replied, looking up. "I am alone. I came by myself on a whim."

"It's quite chilly this evening," he said, stepping down once. They started down the stairs beside each other. "Would you fancy a cup of coffee, by chance, before making your way home?"

Gretchen smiled. He certainly had a forward manner; but she found it refreshing, and—after all, she had really been seeking him, had she not? "Why, that sounds like a delightful diversion, Professor. I believe I shall."

With that, they set off together across the plaza. Gretchen started immediately upon a likely topic of conversation: the concert they had just attended. It was instantly evident that Professor Bridwell had found the Liszt etudes as breathtaking as she had. And during the Vivaldi, as well, he agreed that he had felt a sudden chill at precisely the same time as she.

"The ensemble did well," she concluded. "I suppose that is the way Vivaldi would have heard the work too—none of these large, modern orchestras quite out of proportion to the delicacy of the music."

"The modern orchestra," stated the professor, "is well enough suited for modern works, but really, the intimacy required for performing earlier works—as Vivaldi for instance—is really lost in the great crowd of strings."

"Agreed."

Presently they came to the campus gates and found their way to a small café. Seated at a tiny marble table, they had a delightful tête-à-tête, and found much to agree upon regarding both the performance, and the subject of music in general. Though he had not quite her madness for Liszt, he agreed with Gretchen's assessment of the "Transcendental Etudes"—divinely inspired, and, like much of Liszt's work, nearly beyond the reach of mortals.

Gretchen was on her second coffee and feeling rather giddy. She could hardly hold her cup steady, and she finally set it down with a laugh.

"Do you play an instrument, Professor?" she asked, pushing her cup away with one hand.

"Well, I would not so much call it playing the instrument," he answered, "as playing _at_ the instrument."

"I see," she laughed. "Rather the way I play _at_ the viola—though I daresay you speak of Liszt's writing as if you have some experience with it."

The professor seemed rather at a loss for an instant. He glanced away over Gretchen's shoulder, but recalled himself quickly and lifted his cup to his lips, meeting her eyes again. "I do admit I have _tried_." He set his cup down while reaching into his vest pocket, as if searching for something. "But really," he continued, "I haven't the technique. How about yourself, Miss Haviland? I take it you do rather well yourself, upon the viola."

Gretchen blushed, realizing that she must have sounded boastful just then. The professor seemed not to have taken it in stride—she realized that this must have accounted for his momentary loss for words. "Well," she said then, settling herself forward upon her chair. "At one time—when I was quite young, you understand—I fancied I would perform upon the instrument. But..."

"Ah." Professor Bridwell smiled. "Then, other interests swept you away, no doubt. But still you play?" He had pulled a silver cigarette case from his vest pocket, and he turned it over in his fingers.

"Oh, indeed." Gretchen sighed deeply. "I suppose, with all modesty set aside, I was adequate on the instrument—but adequacy in a performer is hardly to be tolerated..." Before he could reply, she rushed onward, feeling her face flush. "I certainly do not practice with any regularity of late!"

Professor Bridwell laughed. "I daresay—at our time of life—leisure hours seem so unobtainable..." He looked at his cigarette case, polishing it with a thumb. Seeming to think better of smoking just then, however, he returned the case to his vest pocket.

Gretchen's smile was thin. She inclined her head, acknowledging the truth of what he said—they were indeed probably of an age. Certainly, she thought he could be no more than thirty-three or thereabouts. "Then, too, music, while an engaging diversion, and the source of much happiness, is better shared, wouldn't you say Professor?" He nodded slightly, and Gretchen clarified her statement. "That is to say—practicing is all very well, but...the joy of music is in sharing it with one's friends—musical soirées and evenings in the parlor with a roaring fire. Old friends gathered around the piano—and champagne!—"

Professor Bridwell warmed to her words, and rubbed his hands together as if before the very fire she had mentioned. "You have hit it precisely," he replied with enthusiasm. "Why—it's no wonder that living, as I do, alone in a house that I fear is far too large for..."

Gretchen thought she detected the professor falter just then, and there was the slightest of pauses in his speech.

"... For myself alone, you see," he finished. He laughed at himself, tossing the black mop of hair to one side. "But I needed some place instantly when I arrived here. I will probably find smaller digs in a year or so, when I've come to know the city more intimately."

"Indeed," Gretchen answered, returning his smile. "I quite understand how one needs permanent lodgings—the more quickly one can find them in a strange city, why, the quicker one is able to settle into life, get one's bearings in a foreign port."

"So true," he replied with a firm nod.

A few moments later, a juncture seemed to have been reached in their conversation. Their coffees were at an end, and neither of them had touched their cups for what seemed ages, so engaged had they become in their conversation.

"But now," Professor Bridwell exclaimed, with a glance to his pocket watch, "I should not be keeping you away from your supper or—or your other duties any longer. Please allow me to escort you home, Miss Haviland—or where you may be going."

"Thank you, Professor—but really there is no need," she declared. She thought that sounded too firm, and she smiled easily, to show that she meant it only literally, not as a rebuff. "My rooms are close by, and the evening air will do me good, you see. It shan't take me more than ten minutes at a brisk pace."

"Yes," he agreed. "I believe I shall walk myself. The air is good for the circulation, as long as one's pace is brisk."

Gretchen rose, and took a curtsey. The Professor held her coat and stood attentively while she donned her gloves. "I do thank you most kindly for the enchanting evening, Professor Bridwell. It—it has been marvelous."

"Likewise, Miss Haviland. I sincerely hope we shall have the pleasure again soon."

With a few more words of parting, Gretchen stepped into the street, followed by Professor Bridwell, and they went their separate ways. She fancied that he stood in the street and gazed at her until she turned the next corner, but she dared not glance back. The evening was extremely cold, though not overcast, and her wool coat, even with a shawl wrapped beneath, did not keep the chill from seeping into her bones. She rarely wore hats, but that evening she wished she had one—one of those large fur hats so favored in Russia, she thought—that would be most appropriate, since she could pull it down around her ears. By the time she arrived at her rooming house a few minutes later, she was shivering. She undressed and went straight to bed beneath layers of feather comforters with a hot water bottle pressed against her chest. She had no appetite for supper, and resolved to arise early and eat a hearty breakfast to compensate.

Sleep was elusive in the extreme, but Gretchen found herself strangely delighted that she could not sleep, for she had the leisure to think over in detail all that had happened that day. And especially, she had time to ponder her interlude with Professor Bridwell. He was a most intriguing man. He was a professor of English Literature—well, that could mean almost anything, she supposed—yet he did not have that _way_ about him. Nearly every professor of English she had ever met—and a good many students of literature as well—were continually spouting clever quotes gleaned from the works of obscure authors, living and dead—they were not particular about that. It often seemed to her that the more obscure the quotation, the more it was admired amongst their cronies. She had always found such practices revolting. But Professor Bridwell was not at all like that. Why, the entire evening—and it had been two hours in fact that they had sat over cups lukewarm coffee—he had never quoted an author, famous or otherwise. Yet, his choice of words, his demeanor, the hint of some foreign influence in his accent—the way he talked of Liszt—all pointed to an intimacy with the most literate form of the English language. Through clear thoughts and meticulous expression—rather than through haphazardly quoting other men—he exuded what she believed was a real professorial air, built upon a solid foundation without pretense. She found him refreshingly attractive, both for his own sake and as a change from the pompous professors she encountered so often in the library. As she drifted into sleep, the hot water bottle pressed against herself, she hoped she would have the opportunity for another such conversation with Professor Bridwell.

Gretchen's cart of books was extraordinarily loaded. Rather than push it slowly between the stacks as she reshelved books, she stopped the cart at the end of each row and carried a few books at a time to their proper places. The library was more quiet than usual, and despite the overwhelming number of books she had to replace that day she worked rather slowly. Lost in thought, she hummed to herself, not so loudly that any patron who happened to be about could hear, but loud enough for her own amusement. She had just returned to the cart and pushed it to the next row. She lifted another armful of books, choosing those whose home was in that particular row, and turned to walk slowly, watching the numbers. She glanced at each book when she shelved it, lamenting that she had too little time that day—there could be no stolen moments of reading, even briefly. She stood on her toes to reach an upper shelf and stopped humming for a moment. The sound of a footfall reached her at that instant, and she gave the book a quick shove.

"Good day, Miss Haviland."

Gretchen looked around to see a fine pair of wool trousers, as she returned her weight fully to her feet. Following upward with her eyes, she felt a pleasant blush. "Professor Bridwell, you startled me!" she exclaimed.

"Careful," he returned, reaching his hand above her head. Gretchen looked up to see that he pushed the book further onto the shelf; she had left it precariously tottering on the edge. "You almost lost one, Miss Haviland."

"Oh dear," she laughed, and grasped the rest of the books more securely to her chest. She continued to walk easily down the row, with her wool skirt swinging about her ankles. "Is there a book I can help you find?" she asked, whirling toward him like a schoolgirl.

"Actually," the professor said, nervously drawing out the word. "I've not come in a—a professional capacity at all today."

"Oh?" Gretchen turned to look at him, but kept walking. With her free hand, she extracted a strand of hair from her mouth.

"The other evening—at coffee," he said, taking up the pace beside her. "Well, really, I found the conversation most delightful and..."

"Yes?" Gretchen stopped, then knelt to shelve another book, lower down.

"And I was wondering," he continued rather quickly, as if he dare not speak of it, "whether you might consent to dine with me this evening."

Gretchen stood up, rather slowly. "I—well..."

"Yes," the professor stammered, "of course—such short notice. I understand. It's hardly proper, and I'm sure you're quite busy. Perhaps another time." He stepped backward as if to take his leave.

"Not at all," Gretchen said with a faint smile. She clutched the heavy books more tightly in her arms. "I should be delighted, really." She caught his eye then, and saw it twinkle. The sight of his smile could not but make her return it fully. "The other evening, it did seem there was ever so much more to say." She continued down the row, with Professor Bridwell beside her.

"Is that an acceptance?"

She laughed and stopped to face him squarely, as if astonished. "Why, I believe it is, Professor." She blinked her eyes. The sudden blush in his cheeks was profound, and she composed herself to keep from laughing.

"Would six o'clock be too late? Or too early?"

"Neither, Professor." Gretchen thought he looked as if he had been handed a Christmas goose. "I'll meet you at the main entrance."

"Stupendous! I'll..." He still sounded incredulous, and seemed near to bursting. He pushed his black locks from his eye, and twisted a lock on one finger. "I'll meet you at six then?"

They took their leaves of each other, and Gretchen thought she heard a faint whistling in the main stairwell as the sound of his boots on the stone steps receded. She flew to her cart immediately the sound died away in the distance. Her unflagging concentration would be required if she were to be finished by six—she had seven more cartloads of books, and less than five hours in which to reshelve them all. She did not stop or rest until five forty-five, when she bid Miss Sadie good evening, and made her way to the main entrance. She stood inside the great oak doors, under stone arches where she could see the professor through the glass when he approached. With a few moments to ponder and catch her breath while she waited, a sudden flutter filled her bosom. Good Lord, she thought to herself—it's a wonder he did not think me scandalously forward. She felt a faint tingling in her cheeks as if she had begun to color. What sort of woman would join a stranger for dinner with five hours notice? Part of her dared not even answer her own question, but another part of her replied that he was not a perfect stranger by any means—she had met him any number of times—and had joined him for coffee with no notice at all. It was hardly the time to start worrying about propriety. She pulled the ribbon from her hair and brushed it before retying the ribbon carefully and flinging her hair behind her back. The least I can do, she thought, is to make myself halfway presentable, though it's a pity I haven't time to change my coat. A hat might have been welcome for its warmth—the evening was sure to be cold—and for fashion as well. But then what is the use of seeming fashionable, she thought, if fashionable I am not?

With his arms wrapped closely around him and his ungloved hands tucked beneath his arms, Professor Bridwell trotted up the stairs. Upon seeing him, Gretchen pushed open the doors and stepped outside.

"Why it's cooler than I had thought," she remarked.

The professor's smile fairly warmed her heart. "Let's hurry along then," he said between chattering teeth, "I know just the place this evening. They'll even have a fire, and if we're quick about it, we might find a table close enough to feel its warmth."

Side by side, they walked out through the plaza. The clouds had descended, muffling the sounds of the city beyond. They continued through the campus gates into the nearby streets. The neighborhood was uncrowded, since so many students had left for their holidays, and though there were a few groups of people walking to and fro, dressed warmly against the weather, only the occasional carriage rattled by. Professor Bridwell led the way into a side street, where they were greeted by a brightly lit café.

"I had no idea...," Gretchen began.

"Of a French café so near campus?" the professor finished for her. "It's quite new." He pulled open the door and the sounds of bustling crowds and gay voices greeted them. "I say," he continued, "the place appears to have been discovered." Gretchen followed him in while he held the door, and stood by removing her gloves while he conferred with the head waiter. She glanced up as she folded her gloves in time to see the man wisk a bill into his apron pocket.

"Follow me, monsieur."

The professor took Gretchen's arm and led her along. Their table was in the back and, as Professor Bridwell had hoped, it was close by an open brick fireplace filled with a roaring blaze of crackling oak logs. She sat in silent attendance while their waiter recited, in heavily accented English, a seemingly unending speech upon the specialities of the house.

Gretchen lost the particulars mid-way, and her eyes strayed beyond him to the fire. "I'm quite overwhelmed," she exclaimed when he had finished and stood poised before them. "Please—do what you think best, Professor."

Professor Bridwell surprised her then, by leaning back with the casual air of one who knows what he is about, and held forth in what seemed, to Gretchen's ear, flawless French.

"Bravo, Professor," she chimed when he had finished. "Your French is beautiful."

The professor seemed somewhat embarrassed then, and smoothly turned the conversation to the decor. The room was hardly what Gretchen should have expected of a French café—it was done in stark white, with high rafters of carved wood, but upon the walls hung gorgeously worked Persian carpets which served to bring the ceiling down and lend intimacy to the room; and to muffle the sound of so many conversing guests. Their entrees arrived in due course—a delightful poached white fish in delicate sauce, which they ate practically in silence, but for the occasional comment upon the food. He asked after her health, and heard the small-talk of the day, then listened with interest to an abridged account of her life, interjecting only occasional questions to clarify certain points. She stopped short of revealing the estrangement of her family, but dwelt upon her years at university.

Gretchen at length noticed the emptiness of her plate and declared that the fish positively melted in one's mouth. Professor Bridwell replied that he would send compliments to the chef. His smile grew gradually as he said this, with a hint of something further he wished to add, but he stopped.

"Was there something else?" she asked, setting her silver carefully atop her empty plate.

"No, nothing," he laughed, putting down his own silver.

Presently, their plates were cleared away and the professor ordered a liqueur with coffee. Gretchen declined a liqueur, having drunk enough wine already to raise her color slightly—she settled for coffee and a small gateau.

"You mentioned that you play the viola," he said, taking up his liqueur with one hand. "Have you been playing long?"

"Since I was sixteen," she replied, stirring cream into her coffee. "I began with the violin as a child—I really can't recall at what age. When I was sixteen I went away for a summer, and..." she stopped to look at him for an instant, tapping upon her gateau with her fork. "Well, I met a young man who played the viola, and I was quite—quite taken with his instrument. It seemed to suit me, really."

"I would say it does," the professor agreed. "Unusual, especially for a woman—mildly exotic even...and intriguing..."

They continued conversing about the viola and the piano, telling each other about their favorite pieces, comparing composers. Gretchen had never played the piano seriously herself—she found it frustrating and was amazed that anyone could master such an instrument.

"It requires such independence of the hands," she said. "I've tried, but I could never play anything worth mentioning. Oh, the organ is another one that I simply cannot fathom. Beautiful to hear, it's quite comical to watch—and seems so awkward to play."

"Neither is really any more complicated than the viola, I should think," the professor replied. He had been twirling his glass for some time, but he stopped and removed his hand from the table. "Think of the dexterity required to control your bow, and the simultaneous imparting of vibrato while retaining correct intonation. It's quite as remarkable."

"I see what you mean, certainly. It all seems easy with long practice."

"Do you sing alto as well?"

She laughed. "Very poor alto, Professor."

"But alto nonetheless. I was certain you would sing alto." He sipped his liqueur again and twirled the glass slowly. "What about opera? I despise Wagner myself."

"Really?" Gretchen replied, reaching for her coffee. "I can't say I truly enjoy Wagner's work, the little I have heard. But Verdi—is luscious."

"Yes, Verdi. I quite agree with your assessment. And Mozart, of course, is beyond reproach."

"Positively. But I generally prefer the intimacy of lieder myself."

"German?"

She laughed and pointed her fork at him. "Not only German—chansons as well."

"I'm relieved to hear it." Professor Bridwell then put one hand into his pocket, and withdrew his silver cigarette case. "Would you mind, Miss Haviland, if I smoke?"

"Of course not," she replied.

"Some ladies find it offensive," he said, opening the case slowly, "but I find it the perfect finish to a delightful meal."

"I couldn't agree more." Gretchen pushed away her plate—the gateau though small, was simply too rich—and sat back upon her chair. Cigarettes had always appealed to her, and she indulged on occasion herself—in private. Cigars she could not abide, however, for they reminded her too much of her father's odious acquaintances—men who came to play cards each week throughout her childhood. "If I might ask," she said quietly, folding her hands the table, "how do you feel about women smoking, Professor?"

He paused, with the open case upon the table before him and looked steadily into her eyes. "Miss Haviland," he answered, "we are living in an enlightened age, are we not? Women's suffrage—and frankly, it will happen soon, I'm sure. University educations—such as your own."

She nodded, but let him continue. He studied the top of the cigarette case with some care. From the side, a hovering waiter produced a shallow ashtray of white china and set it near his elbow.

"I have no objection," he continued, "to a woman pursuing whatever takes her fancy, provided she's reached majority. The same as any man." He fingered the cigarette case, closing and then opening it again. "A strong and independent mind is an asset in anyone, male or female." He looked up hesitantly. "You seem to have such a mind. You've read Mr. Darwin, I believe—and I suspect other progressive thinkers as well."

Gretchen smiled at him, but tilted her head with some puzzlement.

"You once called me more evolved," he replied answering her unspoken question. "That's hardly the sort of phrase an unread woman would use. I presumed you have read Mr. Darwin, among others." He curled his lips upon seeing her amusement and continued speaking. "It is the mind, I believe—and the soul, if one is religiously inclined—that really distinguishes man from the lesser animals. Female no less than male—we all possess that most human of traits."

His extensive reply was more favorable and pointed than she would have thought possible. It pleased her, and confirmed a great deal that she had sensed about him. "Then you won't mind at all if I join you?"

"By all means," he returned without hesitation, holding the silver case toward her. She deftly removed a cigarette, and tamping it upon her fingernail twice, held it out for him to light. She bent back her wrist and let it dangle between her long fingers while he lit his own cigarette.

"Now that we've learned all about me," she said, blowing a thin stream of smoke away, "perhaps you'll tell me about yourself, Professor."

"Please," he said, setting the ashtray in the middle of the table, "do call me Antoine. We needn't be so formal, I think."

She laughed quietly. "Antoine."

"My mother was French," he stated quietly.

Gretchen caught his use of the past tense, but did not inquire further. "No doubt she is the source of your excellent French."

"Maman did speak French to me as a child—but my French is quite poor for anything but domestic conversation."

"From what little I speak," she replied, drawing on her cigarette, "you sounded quite fluent." She let the smoke linger on her lips, then blew it away softly.

"Why thank you for the compliment...Miss Haviland."

"Oh, dear," she said, realizing what she had neglected. "My Christian name is Gretchen."

"Gretchen Haviland," he repeated slowly. "That has quite a satisfactory ring to it."

She complimented him on the quality of the tobacco when they were finished smoking. The hour was past nine o'clock, so they left the café and walked into the street. The fog had descended, lower and thicker than before. Occasional carriages appeared, rumbling quietly along. Tatters of mist blew sluggishly past the gaslights.

"I hope you shall allow me the pleasure of escorting you home this evening?" he asked as they walked.

"I should be honored."

He held out his elbow, and she slipped her gloved hand over his forearm. They walked in silence toward her rooming house, both enjoying the quiet of the evening. It seemed much warmer than before, and Gretchen thought a snow was about to fall. The air had the crisp scent of impending snow.

"I am delighted," Professor Bridwell said after a while, "that you were not busy this evening. Surely you must have so many friends. Other engagements."

"No," she answered, "I have very few friends. But surely—Antoine—there must be any number of ladies who would be far better company..."

"I'm too involved with my books, I fear. Studying all the time; preparing lectures—while the ladies run off with younger rakes." He glanced at her with a teasing half-smile. "I'll be thirty-five come February."

Gretchen laughed to hear him say such things. But she was pleased that she had guessed his age so nearly.

"I fear," he continued, "it is my fate to attend concerts alone, and remain unwed all my life."

"Well," Gretchen replied, "there's something sad in that then, is there not? Two studious people nearly of an age, with no other attachments." She looked sidelong at him. "And with Christmas so near..."

"Yes," he agreed, "there is a bit of sadness in that. Have you no family nearby, Gretchen?"

"No, they're ALL in Connecticut—too far to visit this year, and my rooming house would hardly be suitable for inviting them to visit me."

He laughed pleasantly at this. Yet she did not tell him that she was estranged from her parents.

"Besides my family being far away—at twenty-nine, one cannot be forever running home to one's parents, can one?" she asked.

"I do understand that," he said. "Fancy the two of us then, alone for Christmas—it seems rather a shame."

"It does indeed," Gretchen answered looking away. Snow had begun to fall, silently and hesitantly. The flakes, drifting between the empty branches of trees along the avenue, seemed as large as walnuts; as fluffy as eider down.

The professor laid his hand across Gretchen's gloved hand, suddenly holding her fingers delicately beneath his. She smiled at him, looking at his eyes; his mop of black hair, now bedecked with great white snowflakes. They stopped walking for an instant, and she could see the wisps of mist curling away from his mouth as he opened his lips. The street was silent. He took a step toward her and she realized that she was not looking far up into his eyes—he was not so much taller than herself as she had imagined. She thought—suddenly aware of the palpitation of her heart—she found herself hoping he would kiss her. She believed he would kiss her, just then, and she let out her hot breath. Mist escaped her expectant lips on the faintest of breezes.

They stood for a long moment, facing each other until he turned slowly and stepped forward. Gretchen continued walking beside him with her hand upon his arm. They crossed the street and at last were near her rooming house. She looked up at the falling snow against a gray sky; the tangle of branches above them; the misty pools of light beneath the gaslights. She glanced at his serene face, turning, though she continued to walk.

"I believe you almost kissed me back there, did you not Professor?"

"So, it's 'Professor' again, is it?" He smiled the faintest of smiles and looked away down the street. "Miss Haviland, you did not ask to be kissed—back there." She turned quickly in front of him to catch his gaze, so that he had to stop. "Not in so many words," he added, "I mean—-you hesitated as much as I."

"Fancy that," she replied with a laugh, and began walking again, swinging her legs gaily, letting her skirt billow.

He touched her hand, draped over his forearm, and she felt the warmth of his fingers through her glove. They walked on beneath bare branches and quietly falling snow. It seemed far too warm for snow—tropical almost, as if the gaslights were warming the whole scene—the whole world. Winter was about to melt—the sun might even rise the next instant and spring would return in a blaze of gold and green with soft rain, the scent of flowers.

"In future, perhaps I _shall_ ask, Professor." She leaned to grip his arm more tightly and whispered. "Perhaps I shall."

THE HUNGARIAN LIGHTBULB

When the symphony orchestra collapsed in ruin after years spent floating, half-dead near bankruptcy, all the musicians were thrown out of work. At that time nearly everyone was out of work anyway—many of them discovered soup-kitchens and soon found employment at menial tasks. A few—the lucky or the talented, but mostly those with both luck and talent—found other musical work well below stevedore's wages.

Jurgen had tremendous talent but no luck, yet he could not imagine any other life than being a violist. He would not look for non-musical work—everything was unsuitable, and certainly unattractive. He took the little savings he had and went West thinking to find a place less crowded with hungry musicians. Rather than spend his money on transportation he settled on a romantic adventure: he made friends around the freight yards and rode the rails west until he arrived on the outskirts of a comfortably large city with a clean look—and there he decided to make his home. The city was familiar to him, as a professional musician: it boasted a fine orchestra whose conductor, one Laurence Lamonte, frequently found shockingly intimate details of his flamboyant life splashed across the pages of the tabloids.

In River Street, on the wrong side of the tracks, after hours spent walking from the fashionable districts gradually down the economic ladder into a grimy, dilapidated neighborhood, Jurgen found the Charleston Residence Hotel. Brownstone, four stories tall, it had two windows boarded up on the third floor and unmistakable blackened marks from a conflagration that had never been cleaned away. There was a sign in the window advertising a weekly fee he thought he could manage—if the sign was not out of date. It was yellow, curling at the edges, and could hardly be read behind a smudged window laced with years of accumulated cobwebs. It did not seem like a wholesome place—but the price was right so he walked into the tiny lobby.

"Have you any rooms?" he asked. He had his viola case tucked under one arm and his cracked leather valise dangling from the other hand.

A short, bearded and balding man in a brown, pinstriped suit that might once have been new, stood at the front desk. The stub of a stale cigar not two inches long was stuffed between his lips. He cupped a hairy hand to his ear.

"I asked," Jurgen stated in a much louder voice, "whether you have a room to let."

"Yeah, we got a lot of rooms." The man grinned. "How many you want?"

"One will be sufficient, thank you." Jurgen carefully laid out one week's rent on the counter. "This is a week in advance." The man cupped his hand to his ear, and Jurgen was compelled to repeat himself loudly.

The man swept the money away—into a vest pocket—and handed his new resident a rusty key attached to a length of twine. Scrawled on a paper tag attached to the twine were numbers: a three, separated by a dash from the number thirteen.

"By the way," Jurgen inquired loudly, leaning forward, "you don't mind if I PRACTICE the VIOLA during the DAY?"

"Violin?" the man yelled back, with a dismissing wave. "Just so I don't get no complaints, you do what you want."

Relieved at last to be in some lodging—his last few nights had been spent in damp freight cars, cowering with one or another group of indigents—Jurgen ascended the stairs quietly to the third floor. Room thirteen was the last door on the right at the front of the building. He opened the door after some fumbling with the key. His room proved to be the one with boards on the windows. Only one window, on the left, was not boarded. The inside had been freshly painted, with white paint. The floor was painted a deep gray and partly covered with a threadbare carpet patterned mostly in shades of brown.

Jurgen fumbled for the light switch and pushed it with a loud click. A single bulb glowed dimly, suspended from a long wire in the center of the room. He thought that was par for the course. At these rates, he could not have expected much more. Setting down his valise, he thought he would be in better lodgings uptown, as soon as he found work. He laid his viola case reverently across the raw, wooden arms of the room's single chair. In the far left corner was a single bed. It had no sheets, but a few worn blankets folded neatly at the foot of the mattress. Along the opposite wall stood a sink with a cracked mirror hanging above it, a flush toilet with a broken ceramic handle, and a closet door—again with a broken handle. No towels. Putting his valise upon the bed, Jurgen went back down the stairs to see about sheets and towels.

"This is a residence hotel," the proprietor told him, pushing back the few hairs on his head with one hand. "Sheets in the hall closet at the far end—towels too. Maid comes once a week. Toss your sheets and towels down the chute on Tuesday morning. Don't use too many."

"Thank you," Jurgen replied, making a sincere effort at politeness. He went back up and got a set of sheets and a towel, then made his bed.

Afterwards, he sat on the edge of the bed and opened his valise. It contained underwear, a well-used black suit with tails, a silk shirt, a silk hat, soap and shaving kit, and sheaf after sheaf of printed music. Everything else he had sold as necessary; his cash was securely fastened around his waist in a money-belt. He wondered if there were a trustworthy bank in the neighborhood. Tomorrow, he decided, he would have to go look.

Jurgen surveyed the room carefully before turning in. On the back of the door a relatively new calendar was posted with two thumb tacks. It featured a blonde woman with exquisite, long legs and a coquettish smile—advertising a well-known brand of chewing tobacco. It was the fourteenth of November, he noted. Fifty-seven years ago to the day, his grandmother had arrived in New York harbor from Hungary, dragging two young children behind her—with less money in her pocket than he had. He pondered her memory for a moment—she had been his first musical mentor—then went to switch off the light. He laid down on the bed beneath fresh cotton sheets and listened to the far-off sounds of the city—automobiles and trains, mostly—until he fell asleep.

Early in the morning, just after sunrise, Jurgen practiced the viola quietly for an hour or so. He had no clock, but when he judged, by the sounds in the street that the time was past ten, he left the hotel with his viola case under his arm. He spent the day wandering from street-corner to street-corner in a nearby business district along the river-front and by late afternoon had earned enough money for two full meals. He played mostly Stephen Foster songs—everyone knew them and they never failed to bring smiles. Occasionally a nice old lady would stop, and blushing, ask whether he knew one or another of the favorite tunes of some prior season. As often as not, he had never heard of the tune, but when he did know it, he laid into the instrument with such vigor that they always left a good fistful of coins in his open case.

At a nearby hash-slinging café where the cook had anchors tattooed on both arms, Jurgen ate breakfast. The waitress wore silk stockings beneath a soiled uniform with pink and white stripes—and kept a pencil behind each ear, both of them dull with their ends chewed. Jurgen reflected with some amusement that his description could fit the people as well as the pencils.

The next several days passed in much the same manner. Each evening, rather than hastily becoming a regular at any one café, Jurgen preferred to try all of the nearby places in the hope of finding the most comfortable of the lot. On Thursday evening he saw a small sign he had never noticed before, though he had walked down the same street several times. Neatly lettered by hand in blue upon a white ground—it said simply "Calcutta", with a downward pointing arrow. Jurgen descended the dark stairwell, passed one steel door tightly closed with a padlock, and found the next door unlocked. The same name was painted on the door at eye level. He pushed it open and walked in, thinking he might have found a restaurant a bit more exotic than the typical run of cafés in the neighborhood. The lighting was dim, the decor dark and spare. The place was lined with booths near the door, but opened into a space taken over by a checkerboard tiled floor.

He could see there were only a few customers—not more than five or six people, all told. He looked around slowly, holding his viola case under one arm, the other hand laid across the top of it. He was the only white person in the establishment.

Nobody turned to look at him, but kept right on with what they were doing—drinking and smoking, talking quietly. It seemed comfortable enough—and he saw some things of interest at the far end of the room. There were four tables at that end, under dim spotlights.

Jurgen walked slowly past the booths toward the spotlights. A double bass sat on its side near the wall as if it were the subject of the spotlights' illumination—it might jump up and break into song any moment. An upright piano stood on the left, lurking warily in the shadows, its top opened like a gaping jaw. Jurgen knew this all meant music, and he made his way between the tables to sit at the one nearest the instruments. It was partially shadowed; an unlit candle stood in the middle of the round table—a square table-cloth in white and red checks draped haphazardly, held in place by the candle. Jurgen sat slowly on the nearest wooden chair, facing the music; it creaked when he put his weight on it. He set his viola case on the table and slid it over so he could rest his left elbow on it.

He felt something stir, and looked behind him. A young woman in a sleeveless sky-blue dress approached out of the shadows. Her hair was pulled back tightly against her head, white teeth gleamed in her dark face. She put one hand on the back of the nearest booth, and leaning upon it, spoke to him.

"What'll it be?" she asked with quiet confidence. Her chin rose when she finished asking, and she tilted her head to one side, smiling.

Jurgen gazed at her—she had a pretty face with a narrow chin and strikingly high cheekbones; her black eyes sparkled in the spotlight. He did not really feel like drinking anything intoxicating. "Something soft," he answered. "Something quite soft and preferably cool."

She nodded and shoved herself off gracefully, trailing one hand. Jurgen waited in silence, staring at the back wall. In a few moments, the musicians—three black men in baggy workmen's clothing—returned to the stage, gliding in stealthily, creeping from a door to one side. Without a word, they sat down and took up their instruments. The bass player heaved his double bass upright, then sat upon a high stool and plucked a few notes. The third man carried a clarinet, and standing in the center, whipped his fingers through a few scales without making any sound. They stole a few glances at each other—then broke simultaneously into a molten jazz number, hot as a blast furnace. Jurgen sat back slowly in his chair. The blazing tune crackled and sparked, then settled into a long, burning ember; he could feel the thin layer of ash building up around the coals until it gradually settled into a warm mound of slow heat.

The young woman appeared with a Coca-Cola in a tall glass—Jurgen only glanced at her when she set it down, and returned his attention to the musicians. She slid past his table and strode under the center spotlight—the clarinetist moved to one side without missing a note, nodding at her. She whirled around, snapped her fingers to pick up the slow beat—and launched into song, so softly at first, he was not sure she was singing.

Her voice soon rose in a solo, weaving in and out of the clarinet's melody. Flames rushed up to greet her voice—Jurgen felt the hairs rising on the back of his neck and across his scalp. She sang without words; low tones with all the plaintiveness of an English horn, blending into the ensemble; and at times her voice rose like a whispering flute and broke into autumn leaves, tumbling in a light breeze—the fire crackled behind her.

The splendor of it entranced Jurgen and he forgot his drink, putting both elbows on the table to watch the woman sing. Her voice was so rich, so well-trained and supple—he could have imagined her on the opera stage, singing mezzo-soprano.

The ensemble rushed to a climax that shattered like a glass against stone, and was silent. There were applause from the dark café behind. Jurgen could make out each individual in the audience—pitifully few customers to hear such a singer! He applauded firmly, with authority, and continued until the last clap had died behind him; three more decisive claps and he stopped.

The band played a few more numbers, standard blues fare and a popular show-tune or two—the young woman sang, standing perfectly still with her eyes closed, alone beneath a spotlight. She bowed at last, arms outstretched with a beautiful smile, and strode into the back. The musicians followed her out to take another break.

The pianist lagged behind, following the others to the door, then turned around and sat down at Jurgen's table, pulling his chair close. The man had a few days' growth of beard. He was completely bald—perhaps shaved, Jurgen decided—and his smile revealed one missing tooth and two silver teeth. When he spoke, his voice was deep and bubbly, like a slow pot of soup, simmering. "Don't get many o' yer kind here," he began.

Jurgen flushed suddenly and swallowed, feeling a sense of impending panic. He gaped momentarily, unable to think of a reply. Might it be prudent to withdraw?

The man sat back and laughed loudly, thrusting his thumbs into his belt. He thrust his head forward suddenly, grinning. "I mean—you play that fiddle or jes set yer elbow on it?"

Jurgen felt instantly relieved, and regained his composure. "Certainly I play it," he said, returning the man's smile with some hesitation.

"Maybe you'll play somethin' for me? Maybe I'll buy yer drink, too."

"Well—I—I've never played much—any—jazz," Jurgen said slowly. "Folk tunes, show-tunes—on rare occasions. I'm a symphony violist, by profession."

"Oh," the man answered, wrinkling his brow. "I see. Well, it don' have to be blue—jes wanna see what you got... If it ain't much trouble?"

"Alright." Jurgen pulled his viola case toward himself, and scooted his chair back to give himself some room. He opened the case, strummed the strings once to check the instrument's tuning—close enough, he decided. While he rosined his bow he tried to decide where he should start. He settled on a Hungarian folk tune his grandmother used to play for him. It had a homey, intimate quality; rather simple and easily manipulated. He readied himself and then poured his heart into playing that tune—he worked it around, swished it a few times, tried some variations, caught the fever, and finished off with a fast spiccato variation.

"Sounds like gypsy music," the man said when he had finished. "Hot blood."

Jurgen smiled. "My grandmother—was Hungarian."

"Say," the man said, laying his hand atop the viola case, "why don' you join us awhile? Play anything you like—jes name it. We know 'bout most anything." He stood up and thrust out his hand. "My name's Al," he concluded.

Jurgen clasped his hand. "Jurgen. A pleasure to meet you, Mr. Al."

Al chuckled. "Nah, jes Plain Al. Come on over here..."

When the other musicians returned, the young woman—Al introduced her as Mabel—sat at the table Jurgen had vacated. He took one chair and joined the clarinetist under the spotlight.

"Do you know—uh..." Jurgen paused. "How about 'Nice Work if You Can Get It'?"

"Mmm. George & Ira...," the clarinetist intoned reverently with a wide grin. "Ever'body knows that one..."

They played a seething rendition that soon had Mabel on her feet, improvising alongside Jurgen. She stood facing him, doubling over to peer into his eyes, undulating while they ran on in imitative counterpoint, two fish in a creek spilling down a mountainside. The piano and clarinet stopped while they took the tune up on their own, turning it over, peeking into all the hidden motives, each musically entwined in the other. Mabel was breathless when they finished, and let Plain Al take a solo before leading them all back into the melody—Mabel broke into the last verse and belted it through the room. There were pitifully few customers to applaud.

The place was closing up, and Al sat with Jurgen and the other musicians around a table. They each coddled a tall Coca-Cola mixed with bourbon, and talked and talked, shooting answers and questions at each other like they were playing hot-potato. They were all semi-professional—none of them were paid for playing at Calcutta. Mabel and her brother ran the place, under the eye of a kindly landlord who never bothered them; he came in once or twice a month, sat through a few songs, and left. Mabel and her brother provided free food for anyone who wanted to play for the evening. Times being what they were, they could not afford to hire anyone to play—and had nothing else to draw any clientele. The musicians all held regular jobs, off and on—mostly off, they admitted—and Calcutta was like their own private paradise, where they were real musicians, where people came to hear them play. They were a comfortable bunch, wiling away their evenings with music, going home with full stomachs.

Jurgen felt exhausted—he had been up since dawn—and when he had finished his drink, begged to take his leave. He cradled his viola case under one arm. "I'm wondering, Al," he said as he stood up. "How this place came to be called 'Calcutta'?"

Al laughed. "That's Mabel's idea of jokin' I guess. Mabel, she reads a lot—got some fine schoolin' too." Jurgen did not comprehend immediately. Al flashed his silver teeth and leaned forward with wide, laughing eyes. "Black Hole o' Calcutta?"

Jurgen chuckled. "I think I understand. Good night, Al."

"Come on back soon, Yoorgin," Al replied. "Play some more with us."

"I'll do that." Jurgen put his hand to his head, then remembered he had no hat. He smiled and walked out.

Jurgen returned to his room long after midnight, turned on the single light, and sat upon the bed to look through his sheaf of music. He tossed the music aside after a few minutes and laid down to think back over the evening. It had been a long time since he had had as much fun—sheer enjoyment—as that evening with Plain Al and Mabel. She was remarkable—sophisticated and graceful—they had played together as if they knew each other intimately.

Something fluttered and fluttered against his eyelids—he opened his eyes and looked up. A moth had somehow got into the room, and fluttered around and around the lightbulb, casting shadows that flitted. Annoyed to be cast from his reverie, he took his towel and began flicking at the moth as it circled and circled. Something about the lightbulb caught his attention then—it was unusually shaped. He pulled the chair over beneath it and standing carefully on the chair, looked at the slowly swinging bulb before reaching out to grab the socket. Stamped upon the end of the bulb in rough, smeared letters were three words: Made in Hungary. He almost lost his balance for an instant, and jumped to the floor with a thump. There was an immediate answering thump from the room below, and Jurgen mentally apologized to his lower neighbor.

* * * * *

Two days later, on a Saturday evening, after what had become his accustomed daily rounds of playing on street-corners—Jurgen found himself again descending the stairs into Calcutta. The place was noisier than it had been before. There might have been thirty people inside. He found a seat at the booth closest to the spotlights—the open tables were full. A young waitress in a slinky white dress came over to serve him. He decided to have dinner there—a repayment to Mabel. The last time, he had only ordered one drink, and when he thought back over the evening, decided that he had in fact never paid for it or any of the drinks he had with Al and the others. At least he could give her some business by ordering dinner.

"Where's Mabel this evening?" he asked.

"Huh?" The waitress seemed confused. She let one knee bend, and ran a hand quickly along the strap of her dress.

"Oh," he stammered, "I thought Mabel would be here."

"Oh, she's here," the waitress said, puzzled. "She don' work tables though." She leaned on the table with one hand. "Can I get you something to drink first?"

"I'll have a Coca-Cola."

The waitress left and came back with his drink. She set it lightly on the table, with a battered cork coaster beneath, and slid it in front of him. He ordered a few side dishes—words spilling willy-nilly from his mouth while he glanced over the menu. He was uncertain how much he should order and ended up ordering far too much food to eat alone—but he felt that he really owed

Mabel something. Plain Al showed up later; Jurgen walked over to say hello, and to thank him for so kindly allowing him to play the other evening. Remembering that he had plates of untouched food, he invited Al over to his table. They ate together and talked about the late George Gershwin.

"Pity how he passed away so suddenly, ain't it?" Al observed quietly.

"I'm sure he'll be counted among the greatest," Jurgen replied.

Jurgen joined the band and they spent the rest of the evening working over tunes they all knew. Mabel came out and sang with them, and they rounded out the evening with a few long numbers just for the enjoyment of listening to each other. The crowd seemed more appreciative than it had been before—Jurgen believed that anything would have been an improvement. There were simply more people present, so he felt they were more appreciative, but he guessed it was all part of the same thing they heard every Saturday night in Calcutta. There were a couple of other musicians—a hot young sax player with a large belly and a low-hung belt that barely held up a pair of wool pants with worn knees. There was a wrinkled old man, half blind, who played blues with his beat-up guitar—he had a hole the size of a silver dollar in one shoe and he wore no socks. It was far from the symphony, but Jurgen thoroughly enjoyed his second evening in Calcutta.

* * * * *

Dropping into the Calcutta to play the evening away quickly became a pleasant habit over the next few weeks. Jurgen came to consider his previous life as having been sheltered from some of the finest home-spun music he had ever heard, and he decided there was much to be learned here. Whether they worked in factories or restaurants, or tended stores in the neighborhood, the people who congregated around Mabel all seemed to have one thing in common: concentrated musical talent. They were all masters of jazz melody. He looked forward to his regular visits—an especially welcome diversion after playing all day in the cold, hanging around employment lines looking for symphony work. The pennies he earned during the day mostly ended up in Mabel's coffers—where Jurgen thought they should be. His own savings began to dwindle. He increased the hours he spent searching for good employment.

It seemed to Jurgen that every time he descended the dark stairwell to Calcutta and opened the door, there were more customers than had been there the last time. On the last Saturday night before Christmas—it was Christmas Eve, in fact—Jurgen arrived, thinking he would have dinner there. He threw open the door and found the whole café crowded far beyond capacity. Every booth was full, and there were two new tables plunked down in the corner nearest the spotlights. Every table had an extra person or two squeezed in. The place was like a morning train, but the atmosphere of celebration swirled through the room with the blue haze of cigarette smoke. Jurgen went slowly forward toward the lights—but could not find a seat anywhere. The musicians were out on a break, so the customers all talked among themselves, laughing and cheering. He was about to ask someone at one of the tables if they would mind him crowding in to watch, but Al spotted him from the back doorway.

"Yoorgin! Come in back a while," he yelled, flailing his arm.

Jurgen waved back and pushed his way between the tables. "Excuse me. I'm very sorry," he said as he squeezed through, carrying his viola case over his head with both hands. He made it to the door, and Al pulled him into the back.

"Here, have a glass of bourbon," Al said with his silver-toothed grin. "Christmas Eve's time for a little celebratin'!"

Al brought another rickety wooden chair over to a small table where the musicians were gathered. Seated on one side was Mabel, dressed in a fine long gown that sparkled with red sequins, her hair tied up in a bright green turban; long dangling earrings. She was the picture of Christmas, with a tipsy smile. A chef and two young men in soiled aprons worked the kitchen stove and oven, clanking pans and mixing bowls at the far end of the room; the lights were bright.

"Jurgen," Mabel said as he sat down, "I was hoping you'd be here this evening. I have something for you." She slid her hand into the bosom of her low-cut gown, sending a ripple of laughter among the musicians. "It's a Christmas present," she whispered, fishing deeper and deeper—her shoulders wiggled in mirth. "If I can find it..." She drove her hand deeper to keep them all laughing.

Jurgen pulled his chair closer and held his viola case upright between his legs. Al pushed a tumbler of bourbon in front of him—and Mabel slapped five dollars onto the table with both hands. "Now you go on and take this," she insisted. "Ever since you showed up here, business has been getting better and better. I want you to know how much we appreciate it."

Jurgen looked at the bill—it was a crisp, fresh five-dollar note that had been folded, only once, in quarters. "Thank you, Mabel," Jurgen said, then paused to fumble with his glass. He did not touch the bill, but left it sitting on the table in front of him. "I'm speechless." Everyone laughed.

"Now you just sit here a while with me," she continued. "The rest of you go on out and play for a while. I want to talk to Mr. Jurgen in private." A low murmuring sound swept them, and they backed away. When Jurgen and Mabel were alone, she raised her glass. "Here's to good business," she said.

"To good business," Jurgen replied, raising his own glass and clinking it delicately against hers. "And a Merry Christmas to all..."

"Now that," Mabel said, "is what I wanted to talk about." She spoke quickly, with clarity—as if she had a speech memorized, and was delivering it for an audience. She punctuated her sentences with wispy motions of her long-nailed fingers. "I've been wondering to myself just what kind of man you are. And I've concluded that you're a pretty poor man." When Jurgen's smile suddenly dripped away she stopped and closed her eyes theatrically. "Oh, that was unfortunately phrased. I mean... you're not a wealthy man."

Jurgen sat up straight, and Mabel laughed—then set her glass down on the table. "It takes no Sherlock Holmes," she continued, "to see that. Why, you've been in here nearly every evening coming on six weeks—and in all that time, I don't believe I've seen you in any clothes but the rags you have on now. You must wash 'em, cause you don't smell like my grandpa's barnyard—but I'd guess you don't have any other clothes."

Jurgen felt himself redden, and looked down, swirling the bourbon in his glass until it ran up along the edge, almost flowing over the rim. He should have packed a much larger wardrobe, and left most of his music behind.

"I'm right, aren't I?"

"Al once told me you read voraciously."

Mabel tossed her head and laughed. "Not in those words, I expect. But he's right. And Sherlock Holmes is one of my favorites."

"Well," he answered slowly, "I must admit I'm rather between full-time engagements at this time...and my wardrobe is minimal at the moment... I do own a suit, and a top hat..."

"So I've been asking myself," she interrupted, "how you live, and where you live. I've seen you on street-corners a few times, too. Maybe that's all you do—play your viola—I know well enough it's not just a 'fiddle'. So, where are you living now?" She hung her wrist limply. "Are you on the street?"

"I'm presently lodging at the Charleston."

"Hew!" she exclaimed, waving her fingers. "That place? Nobody of any worth lives at the Charleston. It's full of winos and whores."

"It's inexpensive," Jurgen replied. "The decor leaves much to be desired. But I'm afraid that I'll have to be moving along to even cheaper lodgings by the new year."

"That bad?"

Jurgen nodded. He could probably hold out for another month or two, but by then, he would have to close his new bank account.

"Well," she continued, "the Charleston is bad enough. I just won't stand for one of my friends hanging his hat in a place like that, or worse. Do you need a place to stay?"

He knew she was sincere, but the situation felt uncomfortably close to charity. His grandmother had always warned against even seeming to be in need of charity—let alone actually needing help. "Really, Mabel, I couldn't presume to burden you with..."

"Now, stop it Jurgen," she said with a shake of her head. She scooted her hips forward, cupping both hands around her bourbon carefully as if she were settling in for a serious talk. "Business here has never been better—and I think you've had a lot to do with that. You bring a new sound, and people are paying to hear it, and drink a few, and they're eating food, too... My friend Dotty, just the other day said to me..." Mabel pressed her hand to her breast and forced her voice to a higher pitch, "Mabel, honey, I hear deyz a strange waat boy down at Calcutta—plays jazz on de fiddle."

Jurgen laughed at her feigned accent.

Mabel let her voice drop to its normal pitch. "Are you looking for regular work?"

"Nothing seems to be available in my line."

"Listen. First thing, we have to get you out of the Charleston. Now, my brother's got an extra room—and he's already said he'll put you up, cause I've asked him—any friend of his sister is always welcome. So that leaves work."

"I really could not allow you to do that..."

"Well, hear me out, first, before you say that," she answered. "I'm not half finished."

Jurgen put up a hand to acquiesce. "I'll hear you out."

"My old friend Dotty," she began. "We went to school together you understand—when we were children, anyway. Now, Dotty works for Miss Edna. And Miss Edna thinks the world of her because she's so neat and organized. Miss Edna herself is a flighty thing—she can hardly paint her own lips with both hands."

Jurgen laughed, then bent forward and cupped his glass the way Mabel cupped hers, rolling it between his palms. Mabel had such a way of expressing herself.

"Now Edna's lover-boy is a man named Lamonte. I don't know what he sees in Edna—to look at her you wouldn't think she can do anything right." She winked. "Miss Edna's got something softer than brains; and it's not in her head."

Only the first part of what she said really caught his attention. "You're speaking of Laurence Lamonte, the conductor?" He took a quick sip of bourbon and rolled the glass again between his palms, wondering where she was leading; almost seeing it.

"That's the man," Mabel replied with a firm nod of her head. "With a little help from Edna—getting Lamonte in to hear you play—you'll have something decent in no time." She sipped her bourbon slowly, regarding him. "It won't be difficult."

"Why not?"

"Oh," she replied, moving closer with narrowed eyes. "I know his secret—Dotty told me. Our Mr. Lamonte enjoys slipping off discretely on occasion to hear some... jazz..." Putting both palms on the table, she whispered. "The way I sometimes slip off to sing... Schubert."

Jurgen laughed and sat back in his chair. "Schubert." He did not feel particularly surprised; she probably sang all of Schubert's lieder beautifully. She sat regarding him with a half-smile, and appeared to be finished with her speech. He thoughtfully tapped on his glass a few times, mulling over the proposal, gazing at his fingers. Finally, he looked up to meet her eyes. "You know just what to say."

Mabel smiled and reached out to pat his hand. "Be here tomorrow," she replied, "with your luggage, and I'll take you to meet my brother." She raised her glass, and met his in the middle of the table with the lightest of taps.

He sipped. "I couldn't have asked for a nicer Christmas."

"I could say the same about you." She sipped once, then slapped her glass down and stood up, adjusting her sequined gown around her hips, then leaned over confidently. "I'll soon have you joining my secret musical soirées, too." She pointed at the table. "Now, don't forget your five dollars. Let's go make some Christmas music." Jurgen slipped the bill into his shirt pocket, then followed her out the door and into the spotlights.

* * * * *

On Christmas Day at eleven, Jurgen checked out of the Charleston Residence Hotel. Packing took only a few minutes, as he had little in the way of possessions. When he finished packing, he switched off the light and set his valise and viola case down outside the door. Leaving the door open, he went back into the room and, holding a hand kerchief in his palm, stood on the chair to carefully unscrew the hot bulb from its socket. He closed the door behind him, then crouched in the hallway and put the Hungarian lightbulb into his valise, carefully wrapped inside his silk shirt.

CHRISTMAS CONCERT

It was several nights before Christmas, and all along the freeway, cars were lined up like a vast herd of red-nosed reindeer being led off to slaughter. I glanced away from the sight and reached out to snap off the radio. I'd had far too much of the Messiah since Thanksgiving. You'd think a respectable classical station could think of something more original to saturate the airwaves with. But I knew that even if I changed the station, I'd get White Christmas, or Blue Christmas, or Dixie Christmas, or some other form of musical blasphemy. Traffic moved along sluggishly, inching up a long, curving hill. It was raining heavily—one of those sudden tropical storms, only it was happening in a refrigerator. I had the windshield wipers on full, but still I could hardly see the vehicle in front of me.

Along with every other irate father, uncle, brother, and son who was late for some engagement or another, I was in the fast lane. I had gotten caught in a last-minute sales meeting, and I was going to be late for my daughter's concert if the idiot in front of me didn't hurry up. The offending car was a Jeep, jacked up on all fours with tires big enough to dwarf a road-grader, and had struts and shock absorbers and what-not sticking out all over the undercarriage—a real useful piece of machinery for navigating the treacherous Silicon Valley freeways: when you see a car you don't like, you just roll right over it. The Jeep had one of those typical California vanity plates, held in place by a brass frame which, had I been able to read it in the dark, would have said "My other truck is a Mack." The driver was pumping on his brakes continually, no doubt keeping time to some Country Christmas Hit Classic. Lounging on top of this pinnacle of western automotive engineering was a Christmas tree, lashed with a couple pieces of thin twine—probably on its way to a living room hung with paintings of nudes on black velvet, and soon to be littered with tacky country decorations and strings of popcorn. The tree listed to one side, bobbing over the edge of the Jeep's roof in time with the blinking brake lights. The driver's girlfriend was smooching up to him in the front seat—I could see her outline through the back window, practically sitting in his lap... maybe she _was_ in his lap. I started thinking they probably deserved to lose the whole tree. They'd have a real nice surprise when they got home without it.

I reached over to turn on the radio again, thinking the hourly excerpt from the Messiah might be over by then. I should have brought a tape from home, but I'd barely had time to change my suit. Just when my eyes were averted for an instant, the Christmas-tree bedecked vehicle in front of me decided to drop its load. I felt my car go bump, bump, and slammed on my brakes before I even looked up. The car behind me skidded and swerved to one side, then leaned on his horn as if he'd run into an iceberg. I just hit the emergency lights and leaned on my own horn. The guy in front, perhaps hearing the tooting chorus behind him, stopped just down the road, and like an idiot, put his Jeep into reverse and came hurtling back toward me. He skidded to a stop and put on his emergency lights.

What kind of jerk ties down a Christmas tree so loosely that it flops off in the middle of a freeway? We were only doing twenty miles an hour—in the rain, no less. I thought I would have to get out and check the extent of the damage, and I wasn't happy about slogging in the rain with my dress shoes on. Hallelujah, the jerk stopped, anyway, so I could at least get the name of his insurance company—I'd already memorized his personal license number (which doesn't bear repeating—I'd always thought the DMV had standards of decency).

I hopped out, trying to pull up the collar of my overcoat even though it wouldn't quite cover my head, and started walking forward to have a few choice words with Mister Country Jamboree in the over-endowed automobile. Of course, CJ (as I then dubbed the driver) bounded out of the Jeep and headed my way, tucking in his shirt as he walked. One look at him, and I almost turned around and left—CJ could have been Paul Bunyan's twin brother. He had the shirt to prove it, too: red and black lumberjack style checks, with the top three buttons undone, and chest hair that was thicker than my beard. He also wore cowboy boots and wide red suspenders.

"Holy moley, mister!" he yelled with a tone of real concern. "You alright?"

I was about to lay into him when his gum-chewing girlfriend appeared from behind, tucking herself into his armpit. "Oh!" she squealed, "Ah'm so sorry! Looks like our tree smashed up your brand new car!"

My car wasn't exactly brand new, but I looked around to where she pointed. Sure enough, the front grill was bent in and one headlight had gone out, the glass completely smashed. The tree itself was nestled cozily under the car, nuzzling up against the oil pan.

The look of childish helplessness on both their faces—and frankly what I considered might be a moderate dose of dull wittedness—somehow got to me just then, and I couldn't quite bring myself to swear at them. Besides, the fastest thing to do would be to shrug it off with a happy face, extract their battered shrubbery from beneath my car, and be on my way. I decided that silliness would carry the day. "Merry Christmas!" I called, throwing out my arms. "Sorry about your tree!" Both of them lit up in grins.

"Look—he ain't even mad," the guy said to his girlfriend.

She batted her lashes in astonishment. "We're awfully sorry about this," she chimed, wagging her head.

It only took a minute to get the tree out from under the car. All the while, I was thinking of how to explain it to the patrolman who would undoubtedly appear in a moment: it's just another roadkill, officer, nothing to be alarmed about; I'm sure it happens all the time, what with all these trees swooping down on unsuspecting holiday merrymakers.

The tree was pretty battered up around the lower branches, but it really could have sufficed to cheer someone's holiday—if one cut off a couple feet from the bottom and turned the bad side toward the wall so it couldn't be seen. You only decorate half the tree anyway, right? I started trying to explain this to my countrified acquaintances, but they would have none of it.

"Look, mister," CJ drawled, propping up the tree with one hand. "We busted out yer headlight. Hell, the least I can do is give ya the tree."

The woman tilted her head and shot out a hand to touch my arm. She had a horrified look in her wide eyes that I could see even through her dripping mascara. "You ain't already got one do ya, mister?"

I glanced at my watch and tried to weasel out of it. I'd already nixed the idea of a Christmas tree—told my family (meaning my daughter, Jenny) we weren't having one that year, and that was final. They just shed all over the carpets and had to be tossed out at precisely the right moment in January or the city garbage folks wouldn't pick them up. We'd had a tree one year that sat around well into February because we missed the magic pick-up date. I finally chopped it into little bits and threw it out a piece at a time over the next six weeks. I had no use whatever for a Christmas tree.

In the end, I didn't want to argue with them—it was cold, exceedingly wet, and I was already going to be late for the concert. So CJ helped me load the mortally wounded conifer into my trunk. We groped around for the twine, but couldn't find it, so he battened down the lid with his girlfriend's belt. She had high-tailed it back into the Jeep to wait for him out of the rain. He whispered into my ear while he cinched up the belt. "She don't really need her belt," he said. "I'd have it off her in another couple o' miles anyways." He gave me a wink and wished me a Merry Christmas.

By the time I arrived at the hall, the concert had long since begun and it was almost intermission. I detest arriving late for these things, and I had to wait around the lobby until the first part was over. I was thankful I'd not been any later. Jenny would have been sorely disappointed if I'd missed her big debut: about twenty minutes from the time I arrived in the lobby, she was scheduled to begin her first public performance as a featured soloist—playing "Harold in Italy". If you don't know it, it's a fine piece of music, but it's not in the frequently-performed repertoire, because it's sort of a half-fledged concerto for viola. Not the violin or the cello—the viola: underdog of all orchestral instruments.

My daughter Jenny wasn't always a violist. We started her out right on the violin—something I considered a respectable instrument for a young lady. My ex-wife and I had faint hopes that someday she'd be a concert violinist—Jenny was that good from the time she picked up her first quarter-sized fiddle. We spent a fortune on expensive teachers, and as soon as she was ready, we started her on the long track: youth symphony. But just after her fourteenth birthday, something happened to her brain. I don't mean a premature stroke or some kind of lesion. She came home one day with this hideous dreamy look in her eyes, and she puttered around the kitchen nervously helping me cook. She wasn't talking very much.

I didn't want to probe, figuring she'd tell me what was on her mind when she was ready. "I have to go to Milan next month," I said, trying to be cheerful.

She was tearing lettuce leaves into microscopic fragments, and she looked up. "Will you see Grandma?"

Jenny meant my mother—fountainhead of all family quirks. As a bright-eyed Italian girl of seventeen she married her American sweetheart and came to the States. It turned out to be a terrible marriage, and years later, after dutifully raising four kids, she divorced my father, American style, and went home to the Old Country. Jenny had only met her a few times, but when they did meet you couldn't pry them apart.

"Uh-huh. I thought I might take you along, if you can stand it," I teased. I pulled the salad bowl away from her and tossed in the tomato I had been cutting. "We'll leave the day before spring-break."

She brightened a bit at that, and with a very limp wrist, laid a whole leaf of lettuce on top of the chopped tomato. "Can we stop in Vienna?"

"Oh, I don't know, Jenny... Maybe for a day or two."

She put on a weak smile. "Can we go to the opera?" she asked softly. Jenny's enthusiasm for opera was phenomenal. She must have inherited that from my mother, too—I always thought half the reason she went back to Milan was because they did too many German operas in San Francisco.

"Only if you can drag Grandma along." I picked up the salad and two bowls, then waltzed away toward the dining room.

Over dinner she made her momentous announcement. I had just put a big bite of steak into my mouth and was chewing thoughtfully. I even recall we were listening to something by Prokofiev.

"Daddy, I'm going to switch," she said quickly with an air of non-chalance.

I paused, finished chewing, and then fell right into the pit. "That's fine, honey..." Another pause. She wasn't looking right at me, and I leaned over to try to catch her eye. "You're going to switch what?"

She stabbed at her steak, fork delicately held in her left hand just like we'd taught her all her life. "To viola." She slid a small piece of steak into her mouth and started chewing.

I gagged, and put down my fork, but she kept on chattering with her mouth full, trying to convince me before I could even voice the beginning of an objection. Finally she appealed to my conceit. "You want me to be a great musician, right Daddy?"

I tried to agree that had been our hope, but I was still trying to catch my breath.

"Well, I'm sitting third-desk right now. Do you know what that _means_?" she whined. "I'll never get anywhere in a concert career. You have to sit first-desk—or be the concert mistress."

I coughed a couple more times. "But you're doing fine," I insisted. "You're the best."

She gave me her old half-frown, pulling down one side of her mouth and screwing up her eyes, then rolling them away toward the ceiling. "Daddy," she said, "I'm not the best. Mary is the best." She pushed another piece of steak onto her fork. "I'm sitting third desk with Deadpan Wang." She got that dreamy look again, and balanced her fork on two fingers. "But if I switch to viola—they're always in greater demand you know, because fewer people play viola, Daddy—I could be sitting first desk."

"Look," I told her, "you've already won a couple of competitions, are you going to throw all that effort away, and take up... the _viola_?" I actually gulped.

"_You_ might call it winning," she shot back, "but I've never taken better than second place."

"What about the cello?"

"Daddy," she whined again, putting down her knife and picking up her milk. "The technique is too different—you should have started me on cello ten years ago."

"Does your mother know about this?"

She twirled her fork among her green beans and wouldn't meet my eyes. "No." She looked up with knotted eyebrows. "She doesn't care."

"Jenny, she does too..." I let that trail off lamely and we ate in silence for a while.

Now, I had nothing particular against the viola, as an instrument. Frankly speaking, I've known a couple of violists pretty intimately—and I've always found violists to be warm and tender people. Much less high-strung, so to speak, than violinists. Not quite as passionate as cellists. But I would hardly have considered the viola to be a prestigious solo instrument. How many famous violists can you name? How many great viola concertos? "The repertoire is too limited," I said, speaking what was on my mind. This fact did not deter her determination.

"Mr. Rossi thinks I'd make a great violist," she replied. There was that look again, right in her light brown eyes. Just like her mother.

I had a sudden insight: my teenage daughter had a crush on the conductor. He needed a violist, and apparently he was astute enough to take advantage of a young girl's infatuation to get one. Maybe I'd have a word about cradle robbing with Mr. Rossi. Well, no that was a bit much, I decided. Jenny would have given me the silent treatment for a week. I'd have to stay calm. I told her to think about it for a while, and after a couple weeks, if she still wanted to descend to being a violist, we'd see.

Half an hour later, while I did the dishes, she was on the phone to someone, and jabbered away for a couple of hours to her friends while she dragged the phone all over the living room. I decided again I'd have to join the modern age and get a cordless phone. She probably was about ready for her own private line. I thought maybe I ought to make her pay for it, too.

Jenny worked her way up to first desk within a year of taking up her beloved viola, and despite myself I was beginning to be slightly proud of her. She really was in higher demand, and was constantly so involved with chamber ensembles, youth symphony, flitting here and there, that a lot of her schoolwork was suffering noticeably. Her grade-point average dropped until she was barely maintaining a "B". We had a little talk about that, and decided mutually (or at least I like to think it was mutual) that she needed to pull it up, or I'd pull the plug on all her extra-curricular activities.

So there I was, three years later, pacing the lobby, waiting. I heard applause in the auditorium, so I snuck in the door. The hall was packed solid. At least it seemed packed solid for a moment. I found a pretty lousy seat near the back and plopped myself down while I looked around for something closer. I spotted an aisle seat near the middle, so I moved down and slid into it. I need not have rushed—it was intermission, so I sat there for ten minutes contemplating. Soon, the orchestra filed back in and the audience bustled around to reclaim their seats. The conductor, the notorious Mr. Rossi, reappeared on stage, and the orchestra stood for him. I waited through the next torturous work on the menu, hoping it would be over quickly. When it ended, I clapped a couple of times and hoped the rest of the audience didn't go wild.

When the applause died out, I found I was holding my breath. Then, Jenny appeared in the wings, and strolled forward, her instrument dangling easily from one hand. I could see her scan the crowd and smile—she was really just looking for me. I felt like waving, but that would have been gauche, so I kept my hands to myself. There she was, her black skirt billowing from a waist and hips that resembled her mother's gorgeous figure more each time I noticed it. Her starched white blouse almost crackled. She had spent half an hour fussing over it with the iron, then spent another half an hour getting every speck of lint off her silk skirt. I noticed that her shoe-laces were untied, as usual, and broke out in a smile. At that instant, she tripped over the foot of a music stand—an intense foreboding chill shot through my spine and flashed along every nerve in my body when I saw her sailing headlong toward the floor. A gasp went up from the crowd, and the applause stopped immediately.

Her reflexes, I must admit, were those of a well-bred cat, and her instinct for self-preservation must never have been stronger: her viola never hit the floor. The conductor, wheeling around when he heard the clattering sound, stepped from his podium to assist her in standing again. One of the violinists, whose improperly placed music stand had done the damage, put down his violin to pick up the debris. The conductor had a few words with Jenny, and then he escorted her off the stage. She limped, and would put no weight on one leg. Rossi's arm seemed to be practically fondling her chest and I felt a surge of fatherly irritation. I was already on my feet when they started off, and was trotting down the aisle toward the front of the auditorium.

"I'm her father," I shouted at the old ladies who tried to stop me from ascending the side stairs. By then, some numbskull appeared from the wings to make an announcement that there would be a slight delay, and ask the audience to please wait a few moments. "Tell 'em a few jokes," I suggested as I dashed past. I didn't wait to hear what he said next, but ran into the back, looking for the green room. I was certain that's where she would have gone. I hoped they had a doctor handy.

In another minute or two, I was with Jenny and the infamous Mr. Rossi, who had his arm around her waist and was consoling her in oily whispers. She sat with her priceless viola set across her lap—well, it was priceless enough to me, as I couldn't afford to buy another one like it even if I sold both of my cars. Her bow had been snapped in two and was draped across the viola, two pieces of splintered wood dangling from white horsehair. She wept into the palm of one hand.

"Darling, are you OK?" I asked, rushing up to her. Mr. Rossi wisely removed his roaming hand and stood back a few steps.

"I think I just sprained my ankle," she replied, but that was not the uppermost thing on her mind. "Oh, Daddy—look at my bow!"

"Hey, we can get a new one," I told her, lifting it up. "I saw the way you saved your viola," I said, trying to sound cheerful. "It was a great maneuver!"

She didn't smile. "But... how am I going to _play_?"

I turned to Mr. Rossi. "Look, I'll take her to see a doctor, and..."

"NO!" Jenny screamed. "I have to go on! There are people waiting out there!"

"Honey," I replied, "you have to see a doctor right away."

"Daddy—people paid _money_ to see me play tonight..." She started crying again. "If I don't go on I'll be humiliated forever!"

Under his breath, Rossi was making ecstatic noises in a thick, and quite ineffable, European accent. He sounded like a bad Italian wine with a French label—bottled in Austria and shipped via the Trans-Siberian Railway to Alaska where it was smuggled south on a Canadian ship. "She eez a true artiste..."

Try as I might, I could not convince her to come away with me. She was stubborn in that way—more stubborn than her mother had ever been. Mr. Rossi was no help at all in the matter either: he seemed to agree with her!

"But you can't stand up," I added, still trying to convince her.

"I'll sit," she replied curtly. Her tears had all dried up by then.

"Oh yais, eets no problaim," Mr. Rossi interjected, "we'll seemply yoos ainuther baow." I shot him a look that shut him up immediately.

Jenny insisted on performing. She always carried another bow, and now the wisdom of that practice was proven. Unfortunately, it would have to suffice, though she had repeatedly decried it as being "quite an inferior stick" for playing anything serious. She got her elitism from her mother, too.

Mr. Rossi clapped his hands, entirely relieved. "Ah, but ZEES awdiense weel nevair hear souch subtle deefferense!" I knew what he meant too—the auditorium was filled with hundreds of glassy eyed parents, siblings, and tiny tots; half of them probably could not even spell "viola". Mr. Rossi practically pranced away—off to see the numbskull and make another announcement: the soloist was unharmed; the show would go on.

Jenny had only one further thought: she'd had enough time to stop shaking, but she was so unnerved by the experience that she decided she could never trust herself to play from memory. "I really must have the score, Daddy. I should."

The ladies of the green room were bustling around, trying to fawn over her, but keeping a respectful distance from her father, whom they correctly perceived to be an ape in a touchy mood. Oh, yes, they all agreed whole-heartedly that it would be no disgrace at all. Plenty of soloists had played before with the music in front of them. And considering the state of her nerves, the audience would be so relieved—and honored—to have her play at all, that they would forgive the minor irregularity of playing from the music. By all means, she must have the score.

Reluctantly, I finally gave in and knelt down to tie her shoe-laces. She could not stand unassisted—we tried a few experimental steps and she collapsed immediately under her own weight. One of the ladies produced an ace bandage, so we tied up her ankle, which had swollen so much it looked like a baked yam. A chair was taken onto the stage for her to sit. And of course, since she would be playing from the score, she needed a page turner.

It was the hand of fate: I knew the music, and I was wearing a black suit. "Honey—I'll turn the pages," I offered boldly before anyone else could volunteer. "Just like we used to do."

She gave me that little-girl smile—I'd hardly seen it in ten years, but it made me feel like a real father again. "Oh, Daddy, would you?"

"Come on," I said, putting my arm around her. "I'll escort my princess to her throne." She laughed, and we left the green room with her limping along beside me.

Now, I'm not much of a theatre person. I never attend plays, and the last time I was on stage I was in the third grade. By the time we reached the wings, I knew my face had already turned the color of a ripe tomato and I was sweating. I should have let one of the bustling ladies turn pages for her. How I could face an audience, I had no idea. I concentrated on keeping my daughter's weight off her sprained ankle.

As we sat down, I had a brief moment to look out and feel terrified. The auditorium was dark, so I could only see the first few rows. And I could sense the breathing masses beyond the lights, hovering expectantly in the shadows, ready to slash me to ribbons. A hot wind was blowing in over the bobbing heads in the front; their forked tongues wagged angrily as they coiled slowly. I could almost see the sand whipping across the dunes. They were pretty damp dunes, though, since it was a rainy night. I could feel the intense humidity in the breeze. The conductor gave a nod, with a broad smile in our direction, and the orchestra struck up with the soft introduction.

I panicked at first, shooting my eyes across the page of music, trying to remember what I was supposed to be doing. Where was the first page turn? I couldn't even remember how to read the little black dots. The page took on the look of an obscure foreign document splayed out across the music stand, filled with incomprehensible ink blots. It was a Rorschach test for the incurably insane. The whole scene was backed by the restless, peering faces of the audience. I closed my eyes briefly, trying to calm myself. I snapped them open immediately, however. If I had my eyes closed, I would miss Jenny's signal. If that happened, I knew all would be lost for certain. I'd be laughed off the stage, and she would be ruined before she had even begun.

Only an eccentric maniac like Rossi the Terrible would have picked "Harold in Italy" for the finale of a Christmas concert. It's not seasonal in the least—what was wrong with something seasonal that didn't require a viola solo? But I guess, the orchestra was ready, Jenny was ready—maybe under his mop of stringy and vaguely European hair he thought it would be an exquisitely quirky touch to perform it for Christmas instead of waiting until spring.

The first few page turns passed without incident, and my heart-rate steadily decreased toward normal. She nodded knowingly at just the right instants, and I managed to turn the pages without spilling everything all over the floor or uttering a primal scream. After that, each page turn became easier, and I found that by the time we were well into the piece, I was breathing again, and I could follow the score. I began to get cocky too, and took a few glances at the audience out of the corner of my eye. I could feel the rapture, starting up out there somewhere like a wisp of cool air. She was playing beautifully, passionately. Mr. Rossi was conducting as brilliantly as he could—at least his expansive gesticulations looked fervent. I had heard the piece so many times—the solo passages anyway—that I knew it by heart. But hearing it then, pouring from Jenny's viola backed by the shimmering of Berlioz' orchestration, it took on a sublime quality that I had completely forgotten. It had been a long time since I had really listened to "Harold in Italy", and all the old memories started to come back.

The second movement has a quality like a caravan painted in broad, colorful strokes. It starts out very softly, and builds up as the caravan approaches, passes by the listener, and then eventually recedes into the distance. It's a striking section, and personally I think it's the best part of the whole work. By that time, I was alert again, and was trying to gauge the audience reaction. I had started to recognize individual faces, and remember where they were—I had been turning pages for more than fifteen minutes. I kept track of where people were looking, whether they folded their hands, how they tilted their heads at certain points. I didn't hear a lot of coughing and shuffling either. As my eyes grew accustomed to looking at them, I could see further, beyond the first few rows. They really were—I suppose a Victorian might have said "transported"—by the music. I flipped the page again at Jenny's nod.

I had noticed previously one rather large woman near the front row. She was all dressed up with several long strings of pearls and a long dress of medium golden-brown shades with lacy white frills and a high collar. She had pale, white skin, and her brunette hair was tied up in a hideous bun and topped with a white flower. The whole outfit made her look like an overdressed turkey dinner with all the trimmings and those little white caps on the drumsticks. She seemed for a long while to be even more "transported" than anyone else. I could see the rouge on her cheeks; her lips were parted and she bent forward. The next time I chanced to look her way, near the end of the second movement, she was crying into her handkerchief.

At that moment, as the caravan was fading into the distance, I had a kind of revelation that I'll never forget. This is what it's all about, really, I told myself. This is Jenny's life, and the kind of emotions she can evoke in an audience are her special gift. Maybe I had never really come to terms with the direction she had chosen. I started to feel tingly and blurry eyed. If she, with her playing, could bring tears to even one large woman in a worse-than-average audience, she must also be bringing joy to another, and at least some feeling to someone else; maybe everyone else. If she really wanted to do that with a viola instead of a violin—bringing a new kind of life to a little regarded solo instrument—I felt I could finally accept it. Somehow, over the past three years, my opposition to her taking up the viola had completely blinded me to the fact that she was actually succeeding. It felt like her destiny beginning to unfold. I was sitting on stage with my seventeen year-old daughter, actually participating in her debut as a soloist. How many fathers have that opportunity, I wondered. I felt a growing sense of privilege attending the event, and I was elated by the time the third movement was over. Jenny would fly away from me, of course, into some concert career, climbing ever higher—the inevitable result of a child growing into an independent woman with a great art to unleash on the world. Whether she ever became a famous soloist or not, I thought at that moment, was irrelevant. It was really the ambience that she lived for; not only the brief moments of performing, but also the people around her—the friends with whom she played and passed her time, the practicing, the dedication; even Mr. Rossi, whether I really liked him or not. I could hardly keep tears out of my eyes long enough to turn pages through the end of the fourth movement.

When the music finished and the last blast faded into the walls, there was fully ten seconds of absolute silence in the auditorium. What happened to all the tiny tots? I almost wondered if the audience had gone to sleep! The applause began from the front—the large woman held her handkerchief between two fat fingers, and was applauding wildly, ecstatically, leading the crowd. I had never seen such fervor in a spectator. She was shaking her head, back and forth—I could see the tears glistening on her cheeks—she threw kisses. In an instant, the applause grew to a tremendous roar that crashed against the front of the stage... and then the audience, en masse, were on their feet. I could almost not believe it—a standing ovation for "Harold in Italy"? No, it was all for Jenny.

The reception afterwards was gorgeous. I stood back, still hovering close to Jenny while she took the greetings of her friends and random members of the audience, including the large woman with the handkerchief. I sipped a California white wine that was far too young and sassy, and let her bask for nearly an hour. She still could not stand up, of course, so they had brought her a padded chair from somewhere, and she sat straight-backed like a little monarch, with a big bouquet of pink roses nestled in the crook of one arm, nodding and smiling. The other hand was perpetually extended to receive other hands—and on a few occasions to receive a kiss from some lecherous old geezer.

It ended all too soon for Jenny, I could see. But when I glanced at her face as the last of the stragglers were leaving the room, I could tell she was dead tired. The pain in her ankle could not be masked any longer either. She winced and stretched out her legs when I approached.

"Daddy, let's stop by the hospital on the way home, OK? Just to make sure it's not broken or anything."

I laughed. "Sure thing, Jenny." She had always been small, like her mother, and had never grown too big to carry. I lifted her up, and holding her viola case in one hand, carried her out to the parking lot. The rain had stopped, and half the clouds had dispersed. The moon lit up the remaining clouds like big silver scoops over the far hills—and a few stars twinkled overhead in the cold air.

I whirled around, and around as I walked. "Let's see," I kept saying, "was it this way?" And I would whirl her one way. "Or was it that way?" She was in giggles, with her arms clasped behind my neck.

We found the car—I knew where it was all along, but I was having fun. When we reached the car, I set her down on her feet for a moment to fish my keys out of my pocket. Meanwhile, I handed her the viola case, and she took it absently. She turned around then, and seeing the front of the car for the first time, burst out in a squeal. "What the hell happened to your car?" She limped to follow me to the door.

"Little mishap on the freeway," I replied, unlocking the passenger door. Her eyes went from the front grill back along the side of the car. I couldn't help smiling when her eyes stopped at the trunk. It was half open, with big sprigs of fir tree bulging out all over.

"Oh, Daddy..." she whispered, clutching my shoulder. I heard that warm tone come back into her voice and she embraced me. "You said we weren't going to have a tree this year..."

"Changed my mind, honey," I replied. "Besides—it was too cheap to pass up." I grabbed her viola case out of her hand. "Got it from mah ol' frenn CJ," I drawled.

She looked at me like I was made of goat cheese. "What?"

"Get in, I'll tell you about it on the way," I answered, holding the door for her. "Poor thing had an accident on the freeway, but it ain't nothin' a little amputation won't fix."

Milton Keynes UK
Ingram Content Group UK Ltd.
UKHW032014161124
451262UK00019B/748